For Anaïs and Adrien Lapp

© 1987 Editions Duculot, Paris-Gembloux
First published in Great Britain by
Canongate Publishing Ltd. 1988

British Library Cataloguing in Publication Data

Elzbieta
    Dikou and the mysterious moon sheep.
    I. Title   II. Dikou et le mouton
    mysterieux. *English*   III. Series
    843′.914[J]

    ISBN 0-86214-203-X

Typeset by Pindar (Scotland) Limited, Edinburgh
Printed in Belgium

CANONGATE PUBLISHING LIMITED
17 JEFFREY STREET, EDINBURGH EH1 1DR

DIKOU

AND THE MYSTERIOUS MOON SHEEP

Elzbieta

CANONGATE

Nobody ever heard Dikou tiptoe out of his room.
Nobody ever saw the front door close after him.
But sometimes, in the middle of the night,
Mama would suddenly sit up in bed,
shake Papa and say,
'Wake up Papa, I'm sure that our little Dikou
is gone!'
And, sure enough, when they went to his
room, they would find his bed empty.
Dikou was off again on his travels.

So one night Papa said to his son,
'I'm sick of running after you every night and
I've had enough of your stories. Go to bed and
promise to be a good boy'.
And because Papa looked so angry, Dikou
promised to be good.

But Dikou had just gone to bed when he heard
strange noises coming from outside the house.

Something was crunching,
Something was munching,
Something was nibbling.

'It must be the wind' he thought to himself,
'or the rain maybe'. He opened his eyes.
A strange glow lit up the room.
'It must be the moon', he thought, 'I'll shut
the window'. But when he looked out into the
night, he saw that there was a strange sheep
in the middle of the garden.

Dikou rushed up to his parents' room and
said through the door,
'There's a strange sheep in the garden!'
'Dikou', cried Papa in an angry voice, 'stop
this nonsense and get back to bed at once or
I'll take you there myself!'

Little Dikou went back to his window.
In the darkness the sheep glowed
as if it had swallowed the moon.
'Stop shining like that and go away'
said Dikou, 'we want to go to sleep'.
But the moon sheep just stared at him
and went on chewing.
'I can't let this beast eat up all Mama's
tulips', thought little Dikou, and up he went
to his parents' room again.

But, before he could even open his mouth to
say a word, the door opened.
'Now I've really had enough', whispered Papa.
'You'll end up waking Mama with your silly
stories! Tomorrow you'll be punished, and
that will cure you of this sleepwalking nonsense'.

And, just to be quite sure that his son
would not slip away again, Papa decided to
stay awake himself, all through the night.
But no sooner had he settled in front of Dikou's door,
than his eyes closed and he fell sound asleep.

Just at that very moment the moon sheep
jumped through little Dikou's window
and landed silently at the foot of his bed.
'Are you ready?' asked the moon sheep,
'Climb onto my back, hold tight onto my wool
and we'll go off together'.
'But would we come back?' asked little Dikou.
'Whenever you want to', said the moon sheep.

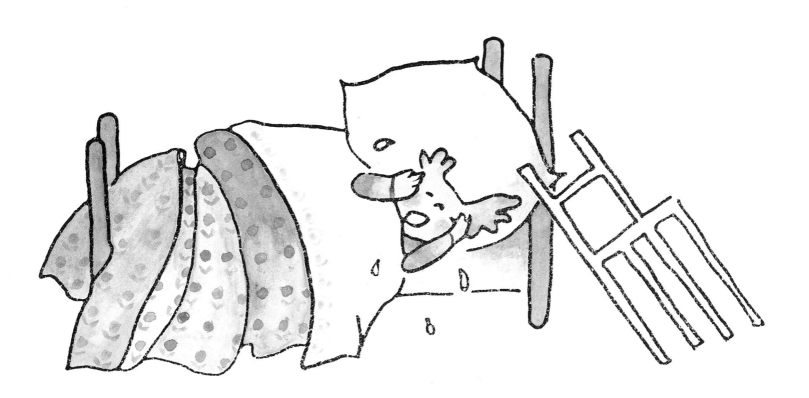

'Oh, it doesn't matter if I never come back.
Mama and Papa don't love me any more',
said Dikou and he climbed onto the moon
sheep's back. Never before had he been so sad
to leave his home.

In the middle of the night Mama suddenly
woke up and ran to the window.
'Papa, quick, help, our little Dikou has just
been kidnapped by a flying moon sheep!'

Mama and Papa searched for Dikou for the
rest of the night. Towards dawn a flight of
wild birds crossed the sky.
'Have any of you seen our little Dikou?'
they asked.
But none of the birds answered since they
were only concerned with their own journeys.

'Oh you bad birds' cried Mama,
'never again will I feed you in the winter'.
Only then did the wild birds answer.
'Don't be angry Mama! We have seen your
little Dikou. He is over there on the island'.

Little Dikou was fast asleep on the island.
He didn't even wake up when Papa lifted him
up into his arms.

Later on when he opened his eyes
he thought to himself,
'One day, one night, I'll see the moon sheep
again. He'll come to fetch me and we'll go off
together to visit the world. But first I'll go
home with Mama and Papa and have
breakfast!'